BEST-LOVED ORGAN MUSIC for Manuals

Book Two

Kevin
Mayhew

We hope you enjoy the music in *Best-Loved Organ Music for Manuals Book 2*.
Further copies of this and other books in the series are available
from your local music shop or Christian bookshop.

In case of difficulty, please contact the publisher direct by writing to:

The Sales Department
KEVIN MAYHEW LTD
Rattlesden
Bury St Edmunds
Suffolk IP30 0SZ

Phone 01449 737978
Fax 01449 737834

Please ask for our complete catalogue of outstanding Church Music.

Front Cover: *A Still Life of Asters, Pears and Apples*
by Berthe de la Baume (1860-1914).
Courtesy of Stodgell Gallery/Fine Art Photographic Library, London.
Reproduced by kind permission.

First published in Great Britain in 1996 by Kevin Mayhew Ltd.

This compilation © Copyright 1996 Kevin Mayhew Ltd.

ISBN 0 86209 811 4
Catalogue No: 1400090

Music Editor: Donald Thomson
Music setting by Tracy Cracknell

Printed and bound in Great Britain

Contents

TRUMPET VOLUNTARY

Jeremiah Clarke (c.1674-1707)
arranged by Alan Ridout

PIE JESU

Gabriel Fauré (1845-1924) arranged by Richard Lloyd

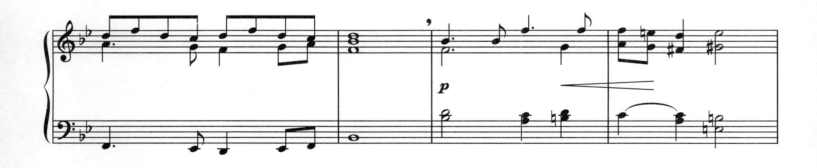

JESU, JOY OF MAN'S DESIRING

Johann Sebastian Bach (1685-1750)
arranged by Noel Rawsthorne

AVE MARIA

Franz Schubert (1797-1828) arranged by Christopher Tambling

CANON IN D

Johann Pachelbel (1653-1706) arranged by Colin Hand

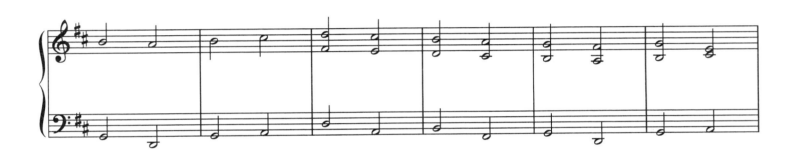

poco rit.

Più mosso

Sw.
8' 4' *mp*

(+ Reed)

AIR from 'Water Music'

George Frideric Handel (1685-1759) arranged by Christopher Tambling

ARIOSO

Johann Sebastian Bach (1685-1750) arranged by Colin Hand

ROMANZA

Traditional Melody
arranged by Colin Hand

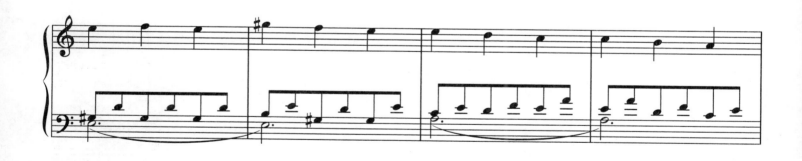

* Change Solo stop if possible for this section

D.C. al Fine

LARGO from 'Serse'

George Frideric Handel (1685-1759)
arranged by Noel Rawsthorne

ARRIVAL OF THE QUEEN OF SHEBA

George Frideric Handel (1685-1759) arranged by Colin Hand